Lizzy the Leatherback

Mike Hamel
Illustrated by Julie Bergeron

Mike Hamel

Published by EMT Communications, LLC
1529 Chutney Court
Colorado Springs, CO 80907
emtcom@comcast.net

First printing—November, 2012

Cover Design and Illustrations by Julie Bergeron
    www.JulieBergeron.com
    JulieBergeron.wordpress.com
    Inquiries@JulieBergeron.com

Interior design, title, and production by Jeff Lane/Brandango.us

You can follow Mike's blog at www.mikehamel.wordpress.com

To my best friend, Susan,
who saw me through deep waters.
- Mike Hamel

To my grandchildren,
who bring a smile to my heart and encourage me
to create stories in picture form.
- Julie Bergeron

A leatherback named Lizzy
swam often near the Keys,
a carefree teenage turtle
just doing as she pleased.

A genus *Dermochelys*
is what you call her kind,
if you're the sort of kid with
a scientific mind.

Now leatherbacks like Liz are
of such tremendous girth
that when it comes to turtles
they're the largest ones on Earth:

the world's fastest reptiles
and deepest divers too;
the *Guinness Book of Records*
confirms these boasts are true.

Bold ridges on her top side,
sleek flippers and sharp beak
gave Liz a stunning profile
and elegant physique.

Unlike the other turtles
whose shells are massive bone,
a carapace like Lizzy's
is hardened skin alone.

Liz used to be a show-off,
but that was history,
for now she had a problem
with her anatomy.

The pain turned Lizzy's spirit
a dismal shade of blue.
It drove her to distraction,
she didn't have a clue . . .

Why was she so unlucky?
How had things gone amiss?
Where could she find some answers?
What evil caused all this?

Could it be germs or fungus
that brought about this grief?
Her friends might have ideas
on how to find relief.

Her pals lived by the coastline
so Lizzy took a trip
into the shallow waters
along the coral strip.

The flora and the fauna
comprising reefs like these,
maintain the eco-balance
in two-thirds of Earth's seas.

These bits of broken rainbows
and cliffs of melted glass
did not make an impression
as Lizzy glided past.

Large schools of darting minnows,
seahorses playing games;
she slinked by them in silence
because she felt ashamed

of looking like an oddball,
with blotched and patchy crust.
Her mates would understand, though;
they wouldn't make a fuss.

Grey groupers Joyce and Jenna
were proud of being twins,
a pair of deep-sea darlings
with matching tails and fins.

"Oh, there you are," said Lizzy.
"I wonder if you might
consider my condition
and offer some insight."

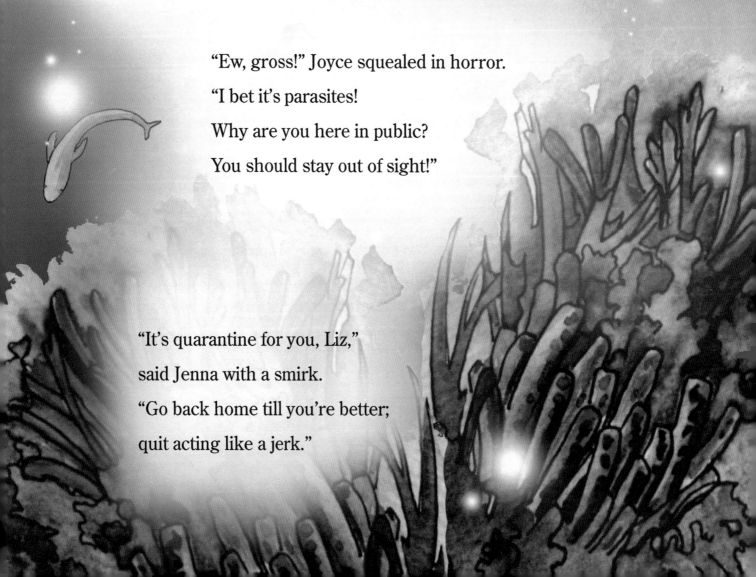

"Don't come too close!" warned Jenna,
as Liz swam into view.
"You could be, like, contagious.
What's gotten into you?"

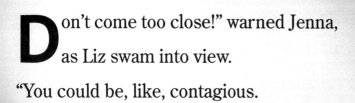

"Ew, gross!" Joyce squealed in horror.
"I bet it's parasites!
Why are you here in public?
You should stay out of sight!"

"It's quarantine for you, Liz,"
said Jenna with a smirk.
"Go back home till you're better;
quit acting like a jerk."

As Lizzy paddled southward
discouraged and alone,
she caught the throbbing beat of
a hypnotizing tone.

It was the pulsing hip-hop
and creamy velvet voice
of Sid the silver snapper
whose rhymes were always choice.

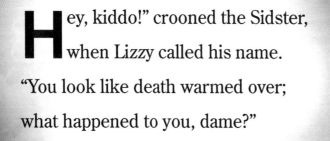

Hey, kiddo!" crooned the Sidster,
when Lizzy called his name.
"You look like death warmed over;
what happened to you, dame?"

"My outside is repulsive,
but inside it's still me.
I sure could use your counsel
and hospitality."

Sid shook his head and muttered,
"My crew will get annoyed.
If you show up at my crib
my rep would be destroyed."

Below the reef Liz brooded
as sky and sea grew dark
and out came nighttime hunters
like Juan the tiger shark.

"*Qué pasa mi amiga?*
Why the *triste* frown?"
"*Hola*, Juan," sighed Lizzy.
"I'm feeling pretty down."

My underside is itchy;
my carapace is sore.
My flippers ache like crazy
and swimming is a chore."

Now sharks are tough and fearsome
and not exactly meek.
Such brutes have little patience
with those they think are weak.

Juan scowled and snapped at Lizzy,

"Complain, complain, complain.

Quit whining like a seal pup;

it's just a little pain."

The next friend Liz encountered,
a parrotfish named Pam,
could chew on crimson coral
and poop out scarlet sand.

The life of any party,
and first-class know-it-all,
Pam stared at Lizzy's features
and cried out, "My poor doll!"

You used to be quite lovely,
so beautiful and strong.
I can't believe my eyes, girl;
tell me what you've done wrong?"

"I don't know how this happened.
My health has gone berserk!"
"It's Karma," Pam insisted.
"That's just the way things work.

We reap what we have planted.

We pay for our mistakes.

There's nothing you can do now;

surrender to your fate."

Her other pals as callous,
Liz gave up and gave in;
she floated on the current
just drifting with the wind,

until she hit a kelp field,
got tangled in a heap,
sank into a depression
and cried herself to sleep.

And that's where Danny found her
all wrapped up in her woes,
and Lizzy felt a nudge from
the dolphin's bottlenose.

Been tracking you for days, Liz.
How'd you get this far out?
For such a bulky creature
you sure can move about!

I heard you're having trouble
and came to lend a fin.
Together we can handle
whatever fix you're in."

You make it sound so simple.
Look closer; I'm a mess!"
Liz slowly turned, expecting
he'd shun her like the rest.

But Danny started laughing
and joked, "It's not that bad.
I've seen far worse on lobsters,
and they're not half as sad.

True friendship's more than skin deep;
I'll stick by you; relax.
No matter *what* you look like,
I've always got your back."

A dolphin and a turtle
swim homeward to the Keys.
And though Liz still has problems,
her spirit is at ease.

Glossary

Callous: Hard, not caring how another person feels.

Carapace: The structure of a turtle's back. In most turtles it is rigid and bony. In a leatherback sea turtle, it is only covered by skin.

Contagious: Describes a sickness that can be passed from one person to another.

Coral: Tiny, hard sea creatures that join together to make a reef.

Crib: A slang word for home.

Eco-balance: The parts of nature working together in a healthy way.

Flora and fauna: Plants and animals.

Genus Dermochelys coriacea: The scientific name of the leatherback sea turtle, sometimes called the lute turtle.

Hola: Spanish for "hello."

Karma: The belief that what people do determines their future.

Keys: The Florida Keys, a region on the south tip of Florida, made up of a group of islands.

Triste: Spanish for "sad."

Quarantine: Keeping people away from others when they have a contagious sickness, so they won't pass it to others.

Qué pasa, mi amiga?: Spanish for "What's the matter, my friend?"

Reef: A chain of rocks or coral near the surface of the sea.

Rep: Short for reputation; what people think about another person.

MIKE HAMEL is a storyteller by trade; the author of the Matterhorn the Brave series and the TLC books for young readers. He has also written several books for grownups available on Amazon. He blogs at OPEN Mike, https://mikehamel.wordpress.com. He is the father of four grown children and the Papa of seven grandchildren.

Books By Mike Hamel

Matterhorn the Brave series:

The Sword and the Flute
Talis Hunters
Pyramid Scheme
Jewel Heist
Dragon's Tale
Rylan the Renegade
Tunguska Event
The Book of Stories
www.MatterhornTheBrave.com

TLC series:

UFO on the Rez
Bezer's Billions
The Long Walk Home
www.TLCstories.com

*Stumbling Toward Heaven: Mike Hamel on Cancer,
Crashes and Questions*
www.StumblingTowardHeaven.com

JULIE BERGERON is a professional freelance artist and illustrator currently living in Arkansas with her husband Charles. She's the proud mother of five children and has twelve delightful grandchildren, all of whom keep her inspiration for illustrating alive. Julie is accomplished in numerous fine art mediums: oils, watercolors, pastels, acrylics, and art clays for sculpting. She also enjoys nature photography and often draws inspiration for her artwork from the dramatic images captured through her lens.

Books Illustrated By Julie Bergeron

Lion Heart & Alessio: The Victory Ride

The Spooky Woods

See Julie's other artwork at www.JulieBergeron.com

Made in the USA
Charleston, SC
03 December 2012